paper parade

written by **sarah weeks**

illustrated by **ed briant**

ATHENEUM BOOKS FOR YOUNG READERS NEW YORK LONDON TORONTO SYDNEY

To my sweet and brilliant friend Nancy Princenthal—S. W.

To Gail, Rachel (who IS the little girl in the book),

and Talia, and my dad, who took me to my first parade—E. B.

Is it a clock?
Tickity-tock

It's a **parade!**
Tickity–tum

With a great **big** round bass drum.

Ba-rum-
pum-
pum

But NO.

Baby brother Joe needs a nap, nap, nap.

Tap–tap

That Joe
is **NO**
parade.

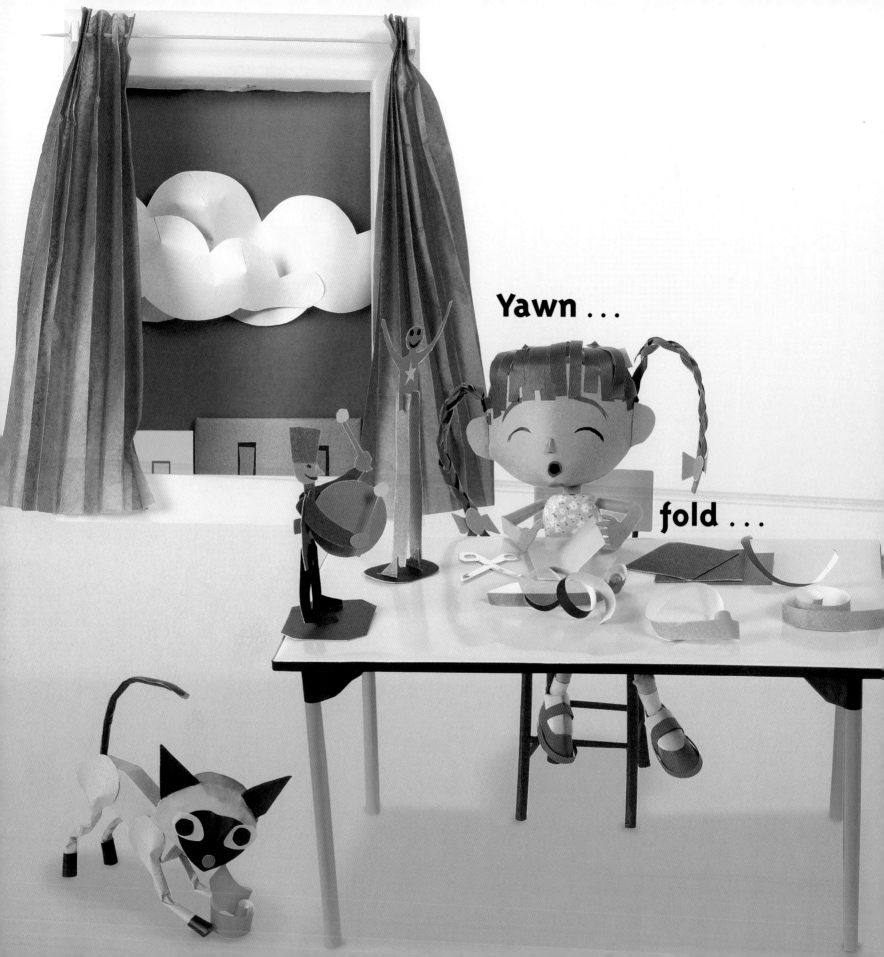

stretch . . .

curl . . .

Tickity-tee

Follow me!

Ba-rum-pum-pum

Here we come!

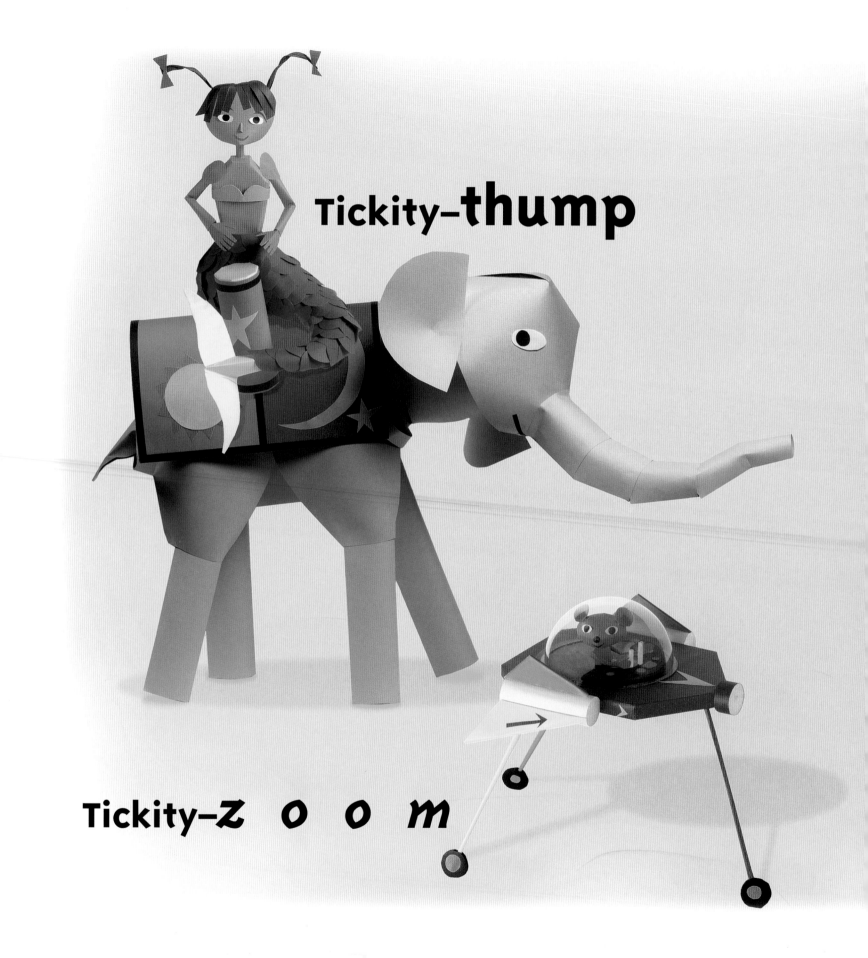

Tickity-**thump**

Tickity-**z o o m**

Tickity-bump

Tickity-boom

Tickity-ting

Tickity-*w h i r*

Tickity-**spring**

Tickity-**grrr**

Tickity-**clang**

Tickity . . .

TROUBLE!

up
up
up
STOP!

Tickity-one

Tickity-two

Tickity-red

Tickity-blue

Tickity-that . . .

Tickity–this . . .

Tickity . . . tickity . . . tickity . . .

Kiss!

Atheneum Books for Young Readers • An imprint of Simon & Schuster
Children's Publishing Division • 1230 Avenue of the Americas
New York, New York 10020 • Text copyright © 2004 by Sarah Weeks
Illustrations copyright © 2004 by Ed Briant • All rights reserved, including the right
of reproduction in whole or in part in any form. • Book design by Sonia Chaghatzbanian
The text of this book is set in Triplex. • The illustrations are constructed with paper.
Manufactured in China • First Edition • 2 4 6 8 10 9 7 5 3 1
Library of Congress Cataloging-in-Publication Data
Weeks, Sarah. • Paper parade / Sarah Weeks ; illustrated by Ed Briant.— 1st ed.
p.   cm. • Summary: A young girl watches a parade from her bedroom window,
then falls asleep and dreams that she has joined the parade.
ISBN 0-689-85607-5 • [1. Parades—Fiction. 2. Stories in rhyme.]
I. Briant, Ed, ill. II.Title. • PZ8.3.W4125Pap 2004 • [E]—dc21 • 2003005473